Make today amazing

Let your dreams set sail

Go with the flow

_____

_____

_____

_____

_____

_____

_____

_____

_____

_____

_____

_____

_____

_____

_____

_____

_____

_____

Follow your dreams

Mermaid kisses and starfish wishes

Dreams can come true

Be your unique self

Ride the waves

Don't ever doubt your worth

Feeling just beachy

Do more of what makes you happy

Dream big

Never give up

Make it happen

Create your own magic

_____

_____

_____

_____

_____

_____

_____

_____

_____

_____

_____

_____

_____

_____

_____

_____

_____

_____

_____

Your time to shine

Always look on the bright side

Dare to dream

Your vibe attracts your tribe

Listen with your heart

Dream, believe, achieve

Explore more

Stay curious

Pass on a smile

Follow your heart

Stand out from the crowd

Spread a little sunshine

Anything is possible

Dream deeper than the ocean

Believe in yourself

You can do it

Let your dreams set sail

Go with the flow

Follow your dreams

_____

_____

_____

_____

_____

_____

_____

_____

_____

_____

_____

_____

_____

_____

_____

_____

_____

_____

_____

Mermaid kisses and starfish wishes

Dreams can come true

Be your unique self

Ride the waves

Don't ever doubt your worth

Feeling just beachy

Do more of what makes you happy

Dream big

Never give up

Make it happen

_____

_____

_____

_____

_____

_____

_____

_____

_____

_____

_____

_____

_____

_____

_____

_____

_____

_____

_____

Create your own magic

Your time to shine

Always look on the bright side

Dare to dream

Your vibe attracts your tribe

Listen with your heart

Dream, believe, achieve

Explore more

Stay curious

Pass on a smile

Follow your heart

_____

_____

_____

_____

_____

_____

_____

_____

_____

_____

_____

_____

_____

_____

_____

_____

Stand out from the crowd

Spread a little sunshine

Anything is possible

Dream deeper than the ocean

Believe in yourself

You can do it

Let your dreams set sail

Go with the flow

Follow your dreams

Mermaid kisses and starfish wishes

_____

_____

_____

_____

_____

_____

_____

_____

_____

_____

_____

_____

_____

_____

_____

_____

_____

_____

_____

 Dreams can come true

Be your unique self

Ride the waves

Don't ever doubt your worth

Feeling just beachy

Do more of what makes you happy

Dream big

Never give up

Make it happen

Create your own magic

Let your dreams set sail